MOLLY
The Beautiful Pig
Meets Totem

Marilyn Ferrett

Illustrated by
Chad Thompson

Once upon a time, Molly (the beautiful pig)
lived in a little house
with Elizabeth, Sam, and Cat (the cat).
The little house was a quiet little house,
except for all the singing,
but there was always enough quiet for a nap!

Everything worked out just fine—most days.
Elizabeth took care of the baking and the tidying.
Sam was the fixer-upper.
Cat was in charge of all the purring that was required
for a happy home.
Molly was sure that it was her job to be beautiful!

Being beautiful was a lot of work,
but Molly was never too busy
for a visit with her friends.
Sometimes, they had exciting news to share.
Sometimes, they had funny stories to tell.
Sometimes, they were sad together,
and sometimes, they would just sing
and
sing
and
sing!

Molly's friends visited every morning.
Robin was always early.
"The early bird catches the worm!" he liked to say.

Rabbit and Frog were never late.
It just seemed that way.

Molly was a patient pig,
but waiting for her friends was easier
and much more fun
when Cat kept her company.
Cat's favourite game was I Spy.

Molly wasn't good at spying,
but she always tried her best.

"I spy, with my little pig eye,
one green frog,"
she often rhymed to herself.

Molly liked to play princess,
when it was her turn
to pick a favourite game.

On a magical day,
she would sit on her velvet throne
and grant wishes
to the birds,
the bees,
and
the butterflies,
if they dropped by.

Cat was Molly's handsome prince,
and if Molly's handsome prince
didn't fall asleep,
she would grant him a wish too.

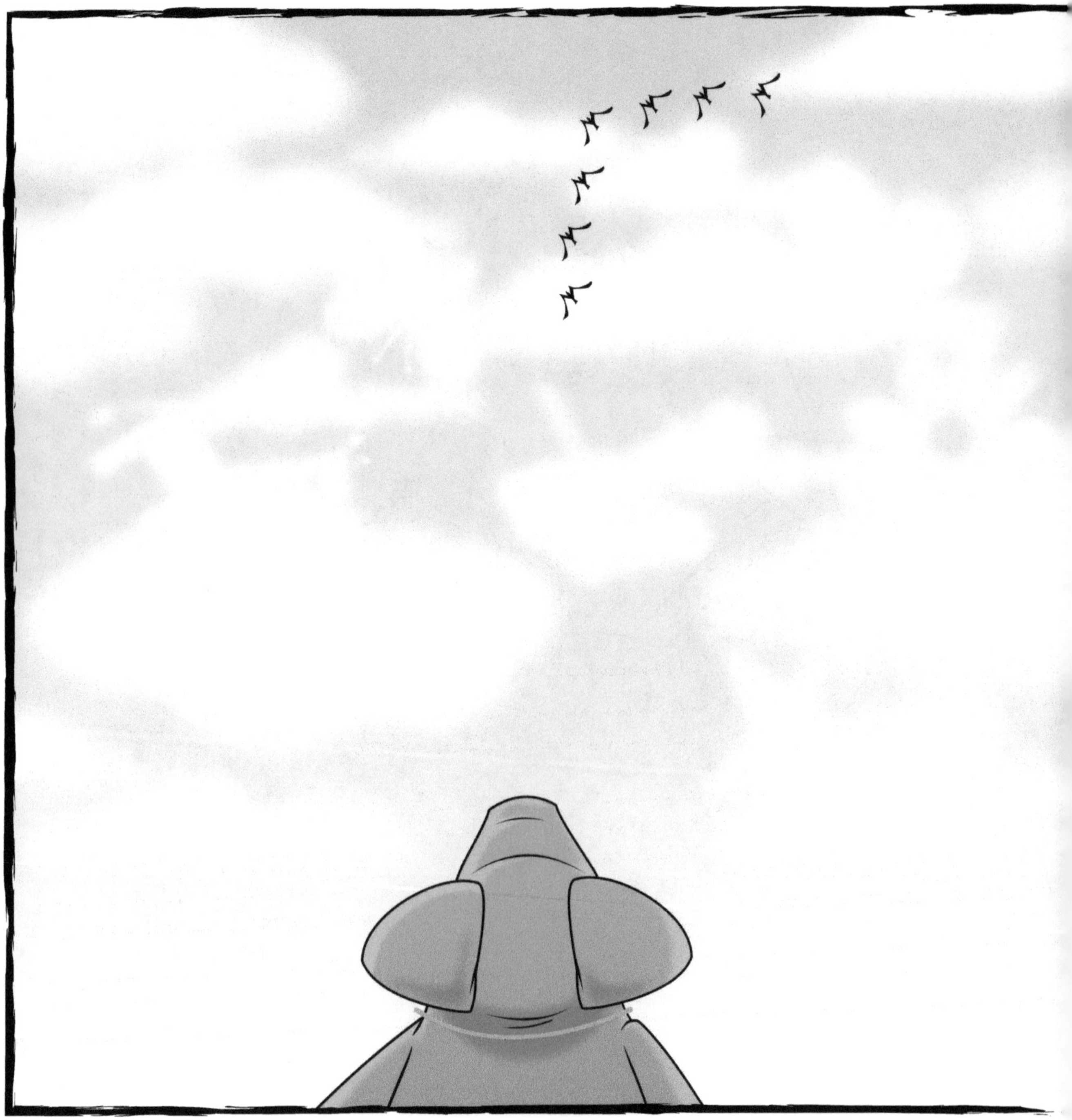

Sometimes, Molly watched the clouds
while she was waiting.

There were ginormous clouds
and shrimpy clouds,
flat clouds
and fluffy clouds,
high-in-the-sky clouds
and just-over-there clouds,
and even clouds that looked like things!

When the clouds were white and fluffy,
they reminded Molly of the fluffy topping
on Sam's ice-cream sundaes.

Sam loved ice-cream sundaes!

This morning, the clouds weren't white or fluffy,
and thunder was rumbling across the sky.

Molly peered into the distance.

There was no sign of Rabbit.
There was no sign of Frog.

Molly's tummy felt squiggly.
Rabbit didn't like getting wet.

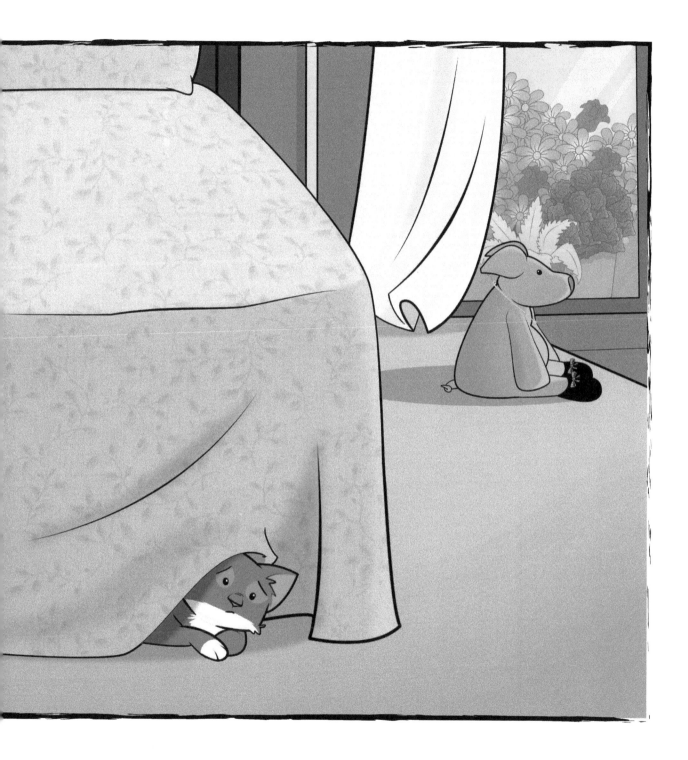

Frog didn't mind getting wet,
but after much discussion,
it was decided
that Rabbit would give Frog a ride!

Scrambling onto Rabbit's furry back,
Frog wiggled himself around.

"Hmmm, this is comfy," he said to himself.
"Hmmm, maybe this is comfier."

"Please hurry, Frog.
The rumbly clouds are very grumbly."

Frog paused.
And then, just like that,
they were off!

There would be no stopping
to nibble at the clover today!

Tiny raindrops danced on Rabbit's nose
as he hopped, faster than fast, across the field.

"Hang on, Frog.
Elizabeth's flowerbeds are just ahead."

Frog was trying his best to hang on,
but his front legs were coming loose,
and he couldn't find his back legs!

Hopping as the crow flies,
Rabbit made a quick zig
and then a zag
around Elizabeth's flowers.

Suddenly, Frog was flying through the air!

THUNK . . . B o u n c e . . . Plop.

"Are you all right?" Rabbit asked,
hopping back to check on his little friend.

"Yes, I am all right, Rabbit.
A blue bottom will look quite splendid
with my green legs, don't you think?"

But Frog was NOT all right.
His blue bottom was hurting.
His green legs were wobbly,
and he was sure that he could see two Rabbits!

Taking Rabbit's paw,
Frog tried to steady himself,
but before he could take a jump,
the rumbly clouds turned inside out
and sent their raindrops tumbling down.

"A cheery song, a cheery song,
a cheery song is what we need!" Robin chirped.

"Yes, indeed," Frog agreed.
"A cheery song is what we need!"

Rabbit gave his fur a good shake,
and then, feeling much more like himself,
he thumped his big back paw to start the beat,
just like he always did.

THUMP
THUMP
THUMP
THUMP . . .

And what a cheery song it was!
Wobbly Frog's low notes
blended with Robin's high notes,
and Molly's snorts and squeaks
sounded just right, in-between.

The warm summer passed,
and every morning, rain or shine,
Molly and her friends would visit
and
sing
and
sing
and
sing!

But this morning, there wasn't any singing.
Rabbit's fur was looking awkward!
Some of it was white,
and some of it was still brown,
as though it knew that winter was coming
but wished that summer would stay.

Rabbit thought he looked very stylish,
in his awkward fur,
but Rabbit's awkward fur reminded everyone
that Robin would soon have to fly away to a warm place
to find his worms.

Frog knew that he would turn into a frogsicle
if he didn't find a cosy pond
to sleep away the winter.

He had been looking,
but so far,
Frog hadn't found a cosy pond that was just right!

The snow piled up, and the cold wind blew.
Winter had arrived!

Keeping each other company,
Molly and Cat played I Spy
and watched the snowbanks for Rabbit every morning.

He was very hard to spy in his new white coat.

This morning, Molly had some exciting news
to share with Rabbit.
A new friend was coming to live in the little house
that was home.
Molly was sure that the new friend was a puppy.
Totem definitely sounded like a puppy name.

Rabbit didn't think that Molly's news
was exciting at all!
Rabbit knew all about puppies.
Sometimes, they chased him
and nipped at his furry tail!

Rabbit wondered if Molly knew all about puppies!

"Did you know that puppies are naughty
and chew things that don't belong to them?"
Rabbit asked.
Molly did not know that.

"Did you know that puppies have tails that wag
and knock things over?" Rabbit continued.
Molly did not know that either.

"Puppies are cute and furry,
but did you know that they make puddles on the floor?"

"Don't worry, Molly," Cat purred.
"Everything will be okay."

Molly closed her little pig eyes.

Perhaps Cat was right.
Everyone loves puppies.

"Good morning, Molly,"
a soft voice whispered.
"My name is Totem.
I hope you will be my friend."

Molly opened one little pig eye,
but thinking she was asleep and dreaming,
she closed it again.

"Good morning, Molly.
My name is Totem.
I hope you will be my friend,"
the soft voice whispered again.

Molly knew all about pigs and cats
and rabbits
and robins
and frogs,
and she thought she knew all about puppies,
but . . .
Totem wasn't furry.
He wasn't wiggly.
He didn't have a wet nose.
He didn't even have a tail to wag!

Totem was a very strange puppy indeed.

Molly wondered if this strange new puppy
liked pink cupcakes
and sunbeams
and cats.
She wondered if he liked to sing.
She wondered if he liked to nap!

But most importantly,
Molly wondered if this strange new puppy
had a kind heart.

Hoping that Molly would like him,
Totem went on with his introduction.

"If something scary happens,
I won't run away," he said.

Molly smiled.

Totem did look very strong,
and he sounded very brave.
Sometimes Cat was a scaredy-cat
and hid under the bed,
but that was okay.

"Whenever you are upset,
I will try to make things better," Totem continued.

Molly was glad that Totem had a kind heart.

Still wondering if Totem liked to sing,
Molly decided that Cat was right.
Everything would be okay.
She was sure that Totem would enjoy singing
much more than barking,
and she knew that Frog would be happy
to have some help with the low notes.

As for her other wonderings,
Molly would ask Rabbit.
Rabbit knew all about puppies!

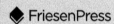

One Printers Way
Altona, MB R0G 0B0
Canada

www.friesenpress.com

ISBN
978-1-5255-2544-5 (Paperback)
978-1-5255-2545-2 (eBook)
978-1-5255-2543-8 (Hardcover)

1. *JUVENILE FICTION*

Distributed to the trade by The Ingram Book Company

CPSIA information can be obtained
at www.ICGtesting.com
Printed in the USA
BVHW022115300722
643448BV00004B/10

9 781525 5254